RICHARD SCARRY

The Big Busy Book
of Richard Scarry

Dear Griffith

I hope you enjoy this book.
I like the story about the cruise
ship best because it reminds me
of our holiday last year!

Lots of love

Letitia xoxo

First published in Great Britain as Richard Scarry's Best Bumper Book Ever in 1991
This edition published by HarperCollins Children's Books in 2008
HarperCollins Children's Books is a division of HarperCollins Publishers Ltd.

1 3 5 7 9 10 8 6 4 2
ISBN-13: 978-0-00-725501-6
ISBN-10: 0-00-725501-2

Printed and bound in China

RICHARD SCARRY

The Big Busy Book
of Richard Scarry

HarperCollins *Children's Books*

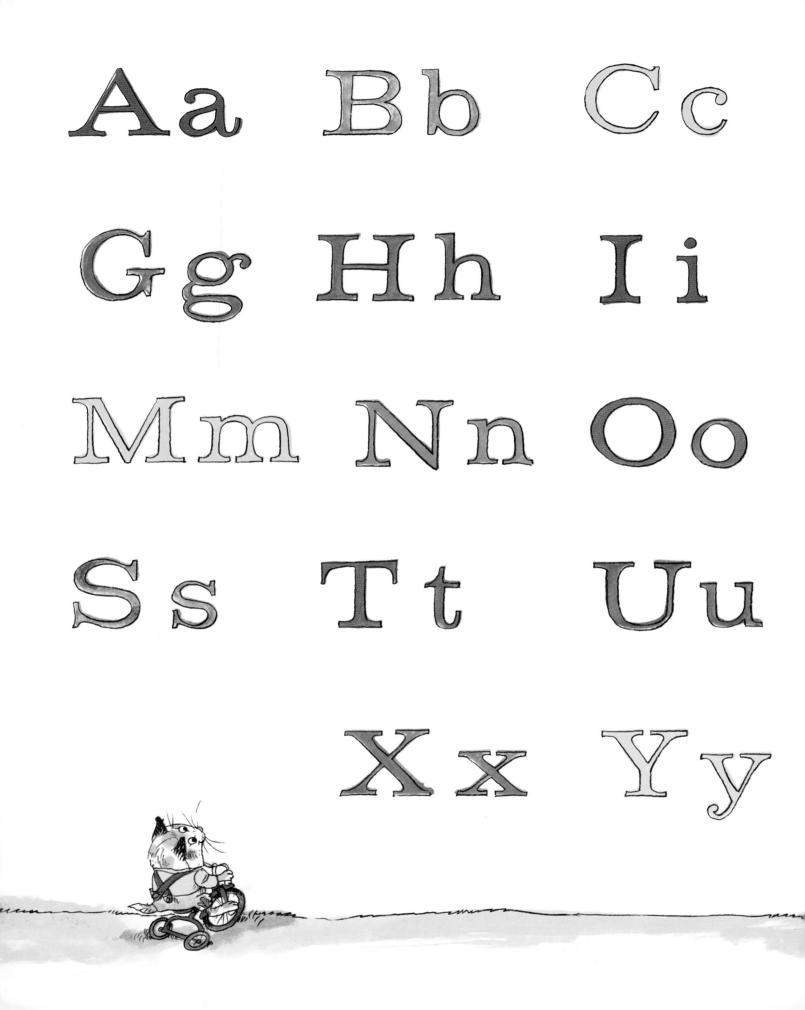

Aa Bb Cc

Gg Hh Ii

Mm Nn Oo

Ss Tt Uu

Xx Yy

jet plane

crane

hook

green bench

wheel

RICHARD SCARRY

ABC
Word Book

bridge

car

BARBER

fisherman

mouse

yacht

submarine

Aa

As Mother Cat was driving Father Cat to the airport, she had an accident.

vintage car

policeman

crane

repair van on the way to the accident

ambulance

hydrant

taxi

attendant

PETROL STATION

arm

umbrella

cane

farmer

hat

a racing car going fast

hay cart

AIR MAIL

MAIL

The dustbin man has a flat tyre.
He is sad.

REFUSE REMOVAL

DANGER

jack

flat tyre

sack of potatoes

bag of asparagus

traffic signal

basket of apples

manhole

farm truck

A B C FARM

CRASH!

car

PARKING

No one was hurt in the accident because
everybody was wearing a seatbelt.

baby pram

pavement

Aa

tail

airliner

wind vane

stewardess

hangar

boarding stairs

tramp

father cat

FOLLOW ME

a flat rabbit

At the airport a plane is about to land all alone. The aviator is landing by parachute.

Hilda running out of the way to safety

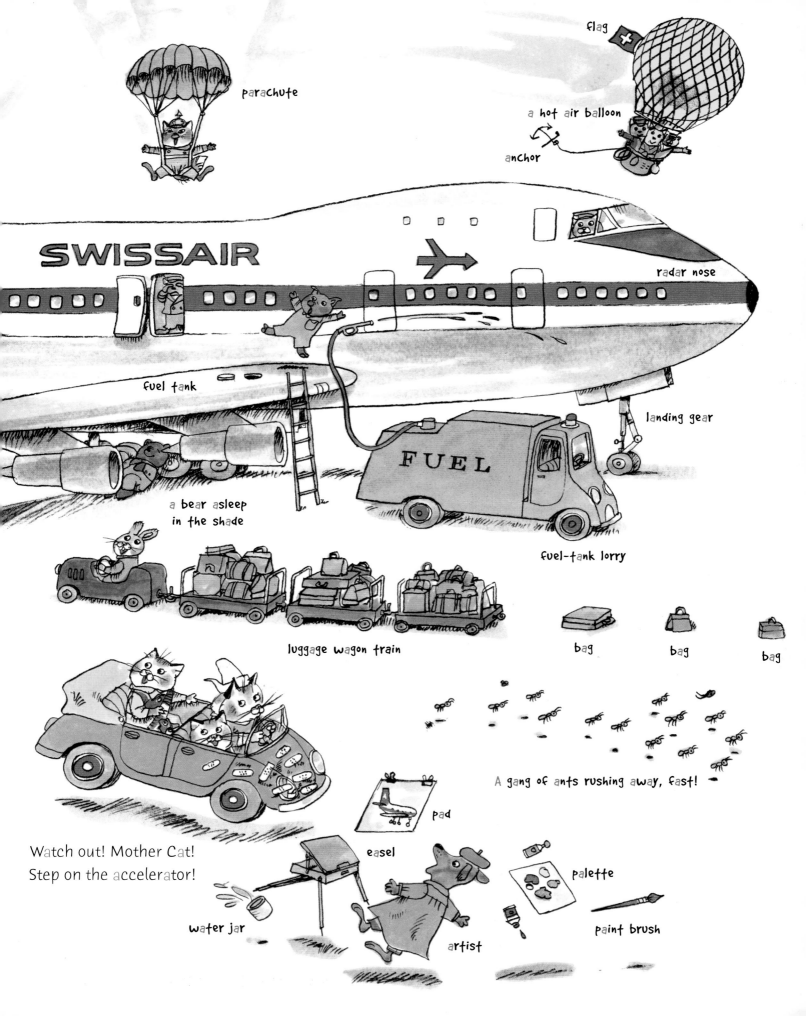

parachute

flag

a hot air balloon

anchor

SWISSAIR

radar nose

fuel tank

landing gear

FUEL

a bear asleep
in the shade

fuel-tank lorry

luggage wagon train

bag

bag

bag

A gang of ants rushing away, fast!

pad

easel

Watch out! Mother Cat!
Step on the accelerator!

palette

water jar

paint brush

artist

B b

boom

cab

banana boat

broken net

bench

barrel

box

bag

bunch of bananas

My, what a busy harbour, with boats all about.

sightseeing boat

blanket

barge

bell buoy

bell

bumper

tugboat

tub

a raised bridge

a brick building

sailing-boat

BARBER

BAKERY

bicycle

boy

bobber

tuba

Captain Salty waves from the bridge
of his big, blue ship.

submarine

radio cabin

book

bow

brush

blouse

boot

broom

bottle

boat bottom

C c

A crowd came to Tiger Cat's picnic.
Everyone licked ice cream cones and
danced to the lively music.

ice cream cone

A couple of mice served cider
from a cement mixer.

cup

Tiger Cat cooked popcorn.
The cover wasn't closed.
Crackle! Crackle! Pop!
Be careful, Tiger Cat!

a cook's cap

POP CORN

packet

cover

can

coffeepot

can opener

camp stove

Rudolf cracked up.

camera

cornet

Crab caught popcorn
in his claws.

accordion

Lowly danced in a circle with a piece of celery.

candle

Clarence couldn't count
the biscuits he ate.

Curly Pig accidentally fell into the centre
of the cake. CRASH!

What a crazy, cuckoo picnic!

Ch ch

It's a chilly day, but everyone is full of good cheer. Christmas is tomorrow. The bells chime in the church steeple.

church

a chimney sweep scratching his itchy chin

CHOICE and CHEAP MEAT
CHARLES CHIMP

The yule log is attached to the sled with a chain.

butcher

latch

chickens

chimney

children carolling

kerchief

patch

Ma Pig is chatting with Mrs. Chipmunk. She is
also burning the chop for her children's lunch.
She is a champion chatterbox.

china

chair

stitch

bench

match

wristwatch

D d

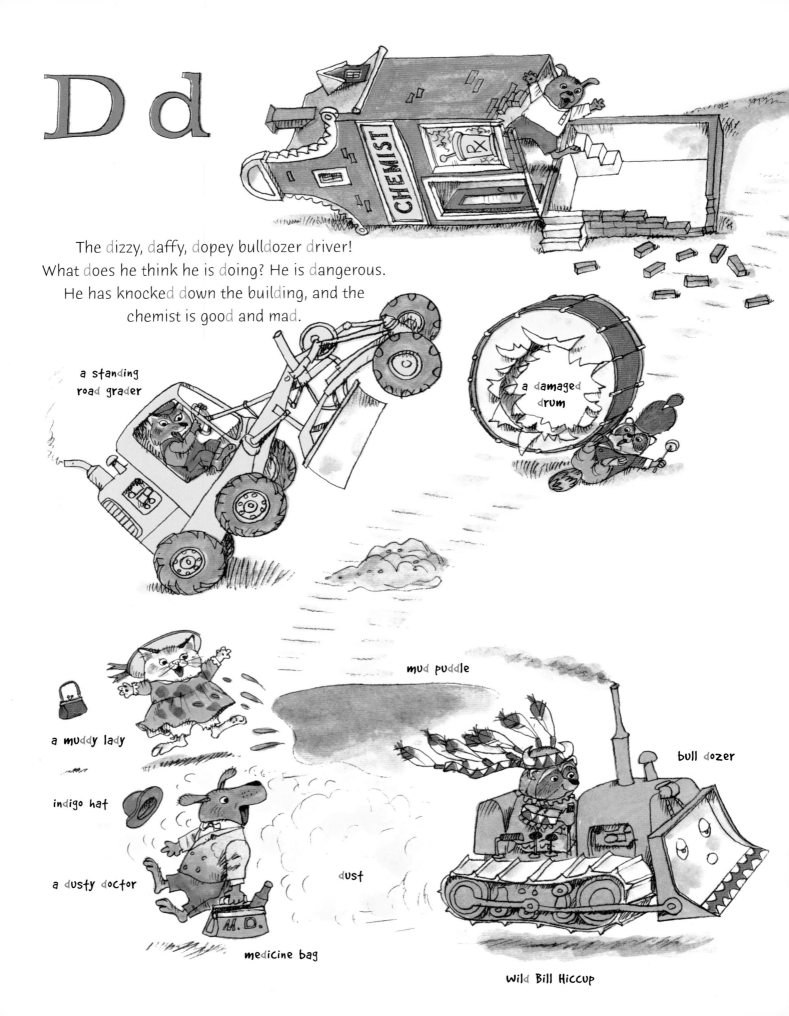

The dizzy, daffy, dopey bulldozer driver!
What does he think he is doing? He is dangerous.
He has knocked down the building, and the
chemist is good and mad.

a standing
road grader

a damaged
drum

a muddy lady

indigo hat

a dusty doctor

medicine bag

mud puddle

dust

bull dozer

Wild Bill Hiccup

DETOUR

a dumped-over dumping lorry

derrick

board

a scared ditch digger

drill

Where is
Huckle hiding?

ladder

a deep ditch

DANGER

door

a dozen doughnuts

DOUGHNUTS

delivery man

E e

Ernie Elephant and his excellent firemen have just driven up to extinguish an enormous fire. Mother Rabbit is screaming for help. Do not fear! They will save her.

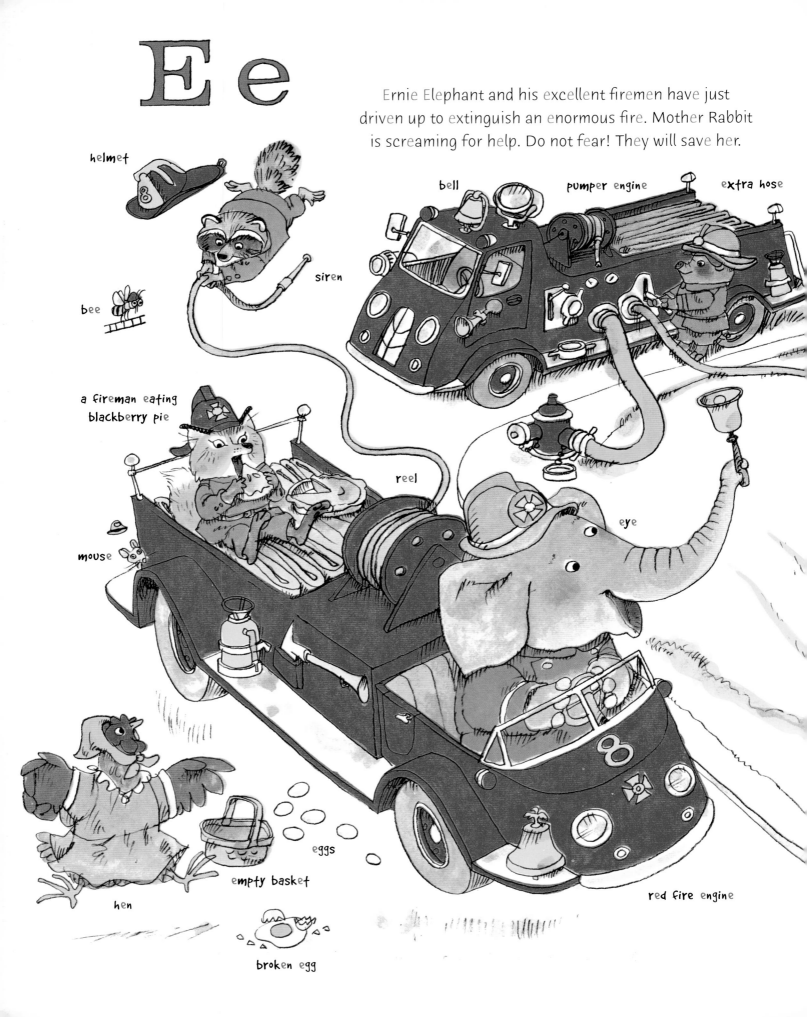

helmet

bee

siren

bell

pumper engine

extra hose

a fireman eating blackberry pie

mouse

reel

eye

hen

empty basket

eggs

red fire engine

broken egg

water

smoke

nozzle

pole

HELP!

HELP!

a leaky hose

green grass

stretcher

50
75
100

evergreen tree

ear

beetle

Huckle

street

Lowly is sleeping on the stretcher during all the excitement.

Look at the three firemen on a leaning ladder. Are they going to topple over?

F f

a fast freight train

giraffe

leaf

a fruit tree

fence

fertilizer

field

pitchfork

Farmer Fox grows food in the fields for his family. There are five furry foxes hiding in the farmhouse. Can you find them?

front wheels

three frankfurters

a funny face

flagpole

flag

farmhouse roof

forest

flower

flow

fireplace

muffins

flames

flour

floor

file

a fat fish

one fly

Five flies follow
each other in a
single file.

Huckle fell flat on his face.

four fish

foot

Wolf and his friend
Freddy Frog.

knife

a floating cap

G g

GREASY GEORGE'S GORGEOUS GARAGE

What is going on at Greasy George's garage?

girl

a great big green lorry

GOOD PETROL

green pump

GOOD PETROL

hot dog

bag

grill

a guitar string

Goofy Goose is going to take a group of gabby goslings to the picnic grounds. Ugh! He is groaning at the thought.

GO RIGHT

a midget car

a gardener by a
glass greenhouse

The telephone is ringing.
B-r-r-i-n-g-g!

a vegetable garden

engine

Grandma is grinning
and giggling.

glasses

globs of grease

Greasy George is greasing a car with his
grease gun. He is wearing gloves.

detergent

glue

sponge

bang!

clang!

Something is wrong here but
the mechanic is fixing it.

Huckle is wearing
racing goggles.

BARGAIN
SALE

CAR WASH INSIDE AND
OUTSIDE

H h

Here is a happy home. However, someone is unhappy.
Father hired a helper to fix the roof shingles and the helper
hit his thumb with the hammer. "OUCH!" he howled.

a head poking through a hole in a hat

heart

shutter

children

hatchet

hoe

Ha-ha!

hose

Huckle has a very high hat on his
head and a horn in his hands.
He is blowing hard.

a hard rock

a helicopter hovering high above the earth

a tree house

branch

Someone is hiding in a heap of clothes.

hook

hanger

hot water

shower

Hurry, Mother! Something is
happening to the spaghetti.

honey

pitcher

dish

ketchup

a hen in
a hurry

bush

Father is digging a hole in
which to plant a bush.

shovel

hole

wheelbarrow

I i

It is a very windy day. The sails of the windmill were spinning around fast until Uncle Irving's kite string tied them up. The Miller is furious. He has an important order to fill.

yikes!

Rudolf's diving high-flyer lost its wings in flight. Rudolf is going swimming with his friends.

pillow

a high hill

pipe

Willy, a little imp, is licking an ice cream cone and spilling it in Uncle Irving's shirt.

wire fence

sails

kite

tail

string

windmill

inn

tourists on a trip

bridge

island

river

sign

NO SWIMMING

a milkman riding
his bike

This is a big accident. In a minute
there will be an even bigger one.

J j

jungle gym

Hilda just jammed a grapefruit between her jaws and went c-r-u-n-c-h. Was it juicy, Hilda?

jaw

jewel

jug

jumping Jill

pyjamas

jumbo-sized lantern

a jet pilot on a joy ride

parachute jumper

Janitor Joe enjoys driving his jeep.

This juggler is juggling jars of jam.

jacket

A joyful jester is playing jolly jingles on his banjo.

K k

The King is having a snack. He is licking a gherkin. Kangaroo is skating in with a cake she has baked for the King. Would you like to share his snack?

a turkey soaking in the sink

king

gherkin

fork

napkin

key

pocket

knife

sock

Duck likes to drink milk.

a basket of crackers

baked bricks

broken leg

Kitten is sucking milk through a straw.

The cuckoo clock goes tick-tock.

back door

keyhole

a mouse peeking through a crack

cook

ketchup

kettle

stirring stick

book

a thick steak

a leaky bucket

cake

kangaroo

a kiss

smack!

pumpkin

skate

truck

Huckle has a pumpkin in the back of his truck.

L l

A large steamroller is rolling wildly over the land.
Look out, all you people, or you will be flattened!

signal light

a leaning sign

a flat limousine

The postman slipped
and lost a lot of letters.

MAIL

a flat bicycle

a flat lawn mower

a leaning laundry pole

a little girl licking a lollipop

oil barrel

leap frog

Mrs. Pig is losing her clean laundry. She calls
out loudly, "let go of my laundry! And please
leave my lovely flowers alone."

telephone pole

a load of long logs

bell

a lazy fellow lying by the railway line

locomotive

shovel

POLICE

a field of flat lettuce

A blue police car is following the silly gorilla in the steamroller.

clothes line

Huckle and Lowly! What are you doing with that loony gorilla?

a tall lily plant

a yellow steamroller

Mm

mouse

midget car

drum

trombone

merry firemen making music

cement mixer

ambulance

medicine

medical instruments

ice cream man

bump!

Doctor Monday on a bumpy road

mail van

milk bottles

milk lorry

bumper

mirror

monkey wrench

mop

motorcycle

monument

WILLIAM TELL

smoke

plumber's van

PLUMBER

Something is the matter with Mummy's motor. A mechanic is trying to make it go. Father Pig is stuck in the messy, muddy road. How mad he is! Oh, my!

a messy, muddy road

SPEED LIMIT 60 M.P.H.

pennant

balloon

a shining sun

anchor

Another aeroplane landed in the pond
– and then another. No more, please.
That is certainly enough!

bench

newspaper

NEWS STAND

a new tie

a painter painting lines

a convertible on a saloon
on a station wagon

Uncle Ned

hydrant

TREE NURSERY

NO PARKING

Oh, my! See how many people have come down
to the harbour to see the boats dock.

GOOD FOOD SHOP

trolley bus

road

Lowly Worm

an old goat looking out of a window

a young goat not looking where he is going

O.K. HOTEL

owl tossing a rope

bow

arrow

pole

soldier in armour

tower

Someone forgot to stop. The boat is going down to the bottom of the harbour.

clock

cannon

shore

wagon

old fort

ogre in dungeon

P p

Pretty Polly Pig is having a party. She is playing the piano. Plink! Plink! All the people are happy.

palm

piano

pot

trumpet

pin

plump pig

platform

piper

plaid

bagpipe

Porcupine goes poo-poo-pa-doo on his saxophone.

piccolo

saxophone player

sharp points

spectacles

parrot

penguin

puffin

pelican eating peanuts

present

a person peeling apples
up in a lamp

peach

pineapple

pear

Peter is pushing Paul.
Stop that, Peter.
Don't be a pest!

plate

a group of pigs

carpet

Huckle slips and drops
the plum pudding. Lowly jumps
up and catches it. Put it back
on the plate, Lowly!

Little Sister pours pink punch
from a pint jug into a paper cup.
Don't spill, please.

plop!

pie

punch bowl

teapot

Q q

The Queen is playing croquet with her friends.
They seem to be quarrelling. Please! Let's be quiet!

The Queen in her quilted robe.

Two squirrels are playing quoits.

Quincy squeezes his water gun and water squirts out.

It hits a squid in his aquarium.

quit it!

Quite a nice shot, Queenie!

mosquito

a quart of milk

Two girls play hopscotch on numbered squares.

7 8
6
4 5
3
2
1

Rr

rudder

G-r-r-r!

rabbit ear

rowing-boat

pirate

raft

drowning Lowly Worm

life ring

Huckle rescuing
a swimmer

Bravo!

The Rapid Rabbits were racing the river Rascals in a rowing-boat
race up the river. The steerer steered right onto a rock. C-r-u-n-c-h!
The race was over. He was in a furious rage.

umbrella

Rhinoceros is rather peculiar.
He prefers not to get wet when he
goes into the water.

raincoat

reeds

rubber boots

a hungry beggar wearing rags

ribbon

radio

a tired rower
resting

carrot

rock

the losers

the winners

A rooster can crow. Can a crow rooster?

outboard motor

rope

water ski

THREE STAR RESTAURANT

raccoon

REST ROOM →

terrace

very bad manners

A waiter is carrying a tray of fruit to a customer.
Who left that chair where someone would surely trip over it?

S s

brush · smack! · stilts · scout · scooter

Daddy Pig came into the house and kissed Mummy.
"What's for supper?" he asked.
"Your seven silly cousins are visiting us for several days," answered Mummy.
"They wish to cook and serve our meals to us. They are making a super surprise supper now."
"Something does smell delicious," said Daddy. "Let's see what it is that smells so good."
Oh! Such a sight they saw!

Sh sh

shade

shaving brush

shell

shelf

sharp shears

a shoulder shawl

wash tub

shoe

What a shame! Mother Bear washed a shirt and it shrank.
Father Bear is blushing with embarrassment.

washing-line

a sheet with shapes shaking inside it

shampoo

splish!

splash!

splish!

splosh!

shower

a shaggy mop

mashed potatoes

A sheep in shabby clothes crashed through the door to
show what his brushes could do. One could even turn on the shower!
Mother told him to shut the door. The cold air was making her shiver.

Children were dashing and rushing
about, shrieking and shouting, pushing
and shoving. Hush, children, be silent!
I mean, hush, children, be silent!

T t

Take a look at the terrible accident. A train has hit a truck that contained ten thousand tomatoes. What a sight!

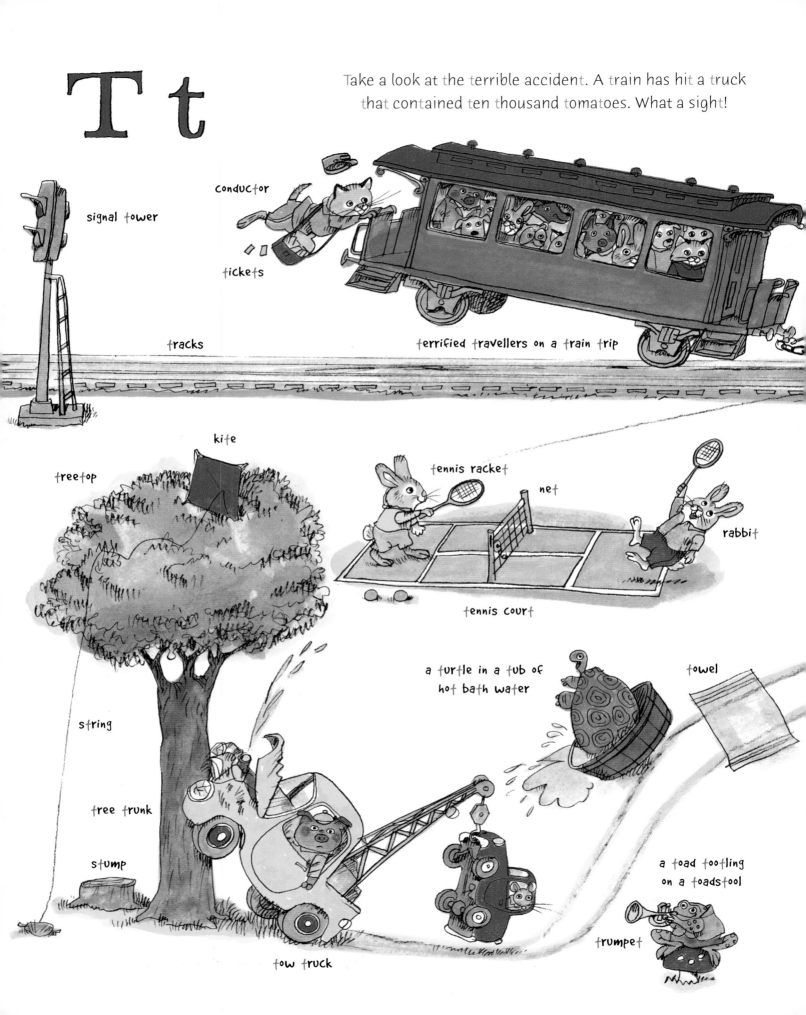

signal tower

conductor

tickets

tracks

terrified travellers on a train trip

kite

treetop

tennis racket

net

rabbit

tennis court

a turtle in a tub of hot bath water

towel

string

tree trunk

stump

a toad tootling on a toadstool

tow truck

trumpet

smokestack

tomatoes

tyres

tennis ball

10

OOT R.R.

a crossing gate torn in two

truck

tent

pot

street

tyre tracks

television set

lantern

stone

table

tepee

Little Sister riding her tricycle

tractor

rut

Rudolf returned to earth too fast and left a great rut
in the dirt. Look! You're on television, Rudolf!

Th th

King Theodore Thaddeus walked down the path without thinking wither he was going. He walked into a thicket of thistles.

thistles

Thrashing about, he found he was stuck to them. This, he thought, is a terrible thing! Then he threw off his thick cloth suit and in three seconds he was free.

However, the weather was cold, and all he had on were thin underthings. It is not healthy to wear nothing but that in the cold.

scythe

Just then Thelma, a nice lady, came along.
"WHAT ON EARTH!" she said. "Something must
be done."

She cut some straw with her scythe. Then
she put a thimble on her thumb, and with
her needle and thread she made Theodore
Thaddeus a new suit of straw thatch. King
Theodore Thaddeus thanked Thelma a
thousand times.

They went back to his castle together, and sat within before the hearth. Then King
Theodore Thaddeus thought…Why not?
Right then and there he asked Thelma to be his queen and share his throne with
him. Thelma was breathless. Nevertheless… she said "YES!"
What do you think of that?!

hearth

Uu

When rain pours down, the ground turns to mud. Uncle Louie's car has sunk under the surface. Tough luck, Louie!

house

The sound of music is coming from upstairs.

Huckle playing a flute

Lowly playing a huge tuba

Crunch! Munch!
Hilda is eating her lunch outside the house.
Down below, a bulldozer is stuck in the muck.

Paul is pulling and grunting. Ugh!

You, there! Hurry up and shut the door before the house is full of mud.

Paddy is pushing.

underwear

Even Rudolf has put up his umbrella.
Too bad he is upside down.

BUTCHER

Aunt Ursula is jumping home after
buying enough sausages for supper.

Duck is busy unloading nuts
out of his dump truck.

nuts

FOURTH AVENUE

a muddy uniform

Sergeant Murphy is shouting loudly, "Don't clutter up the avenue!"

V v

weather vane

aviator

glove

VILLAGE OF LOVE

two chatting wives

A vintage car is driving through a village and over a very high viaduct. This roving family is going to visit relatives.

a van with five jugs of vinegar

1 2 3 4 5

viaduct

a violent driver

river

a brave cat diving to save a mouse

volcano

violets

grape vines

Vincent lives in a cave. He is
shaving his lovely face.

a jolly violin player

Victor, the Viking, is arriving home in his sailing vessel after a very long voyage.

W w

The weather is wild and windy.
The whole town is blowing away.

wig

a window washer
wiping a window

walrus

woods

Lowly worm inside a watermelon

water

a waiter losing his warm stew

wait!

paw

wrist watch

wolf howling at his hat

Huckle wearing a weight to hold him down

a whirring, twirling windmill

a wet towel

a wool sweater

owl growing wheat in a meadow

a girl watching at the window

wrench

a witch in a wheelbarrow

a new wooden wagon

wheel

two fowl squawking

two wiggling wrestlers

a walnut on a wall

X x

axe

A fox and an ox are mixing alphabet soup in a box.
It is excellent exercise.

exhaust

There are exactly six saxophone
players in the taxi.

Yak is playing with his yo-yo.

Why is the little pig crying? He has his own toy.

Y y

yacht

Z z

z-z-z-o-o-m!

a hat that is
the wrong size

bulldozer

blazer

a zebra in a
zipper jacket

Lowly is snoozing.

Chimpanzee

exit   nix

razzle dazzle   yoo hoo

tin lizzie

a dozing baby

buzzer

Yellow stripes show the
safety zone.

Izzy lizard is dizzy. He is walking a zigzag.

RICHARD SCARRY

Funniest Storybook Ever

The Talking Bread

Humperdink, the baker, was mixing bread dough with the help of Able Baker Charlie Mouse. His little girl, Flossie, watched them squish and squash the dough.

After they had kneaded the dough by squishing and squashing, they patted it into loaves of all different shapes and sizes.

Then Humperdink put the uncooked loaves of bread into the hot oven to bake.

After the loaves had finished baking, Humperdink set them out
on the table to cool. M-m-m-m-m! Fresh bread smells good!

Mamma!

Finally he took out the last loaf.
LISTEN! Did you hear that?
When he picked up the loaf, it said,
"Mamma." But everybody knows that
bread can't talk.
IT MUST BE HAUNTED!!!

"HELP! POLICE!"
Humperdink picked up Flossie and ran from the room.
"I must telephone Sergeant Murphy," he said.

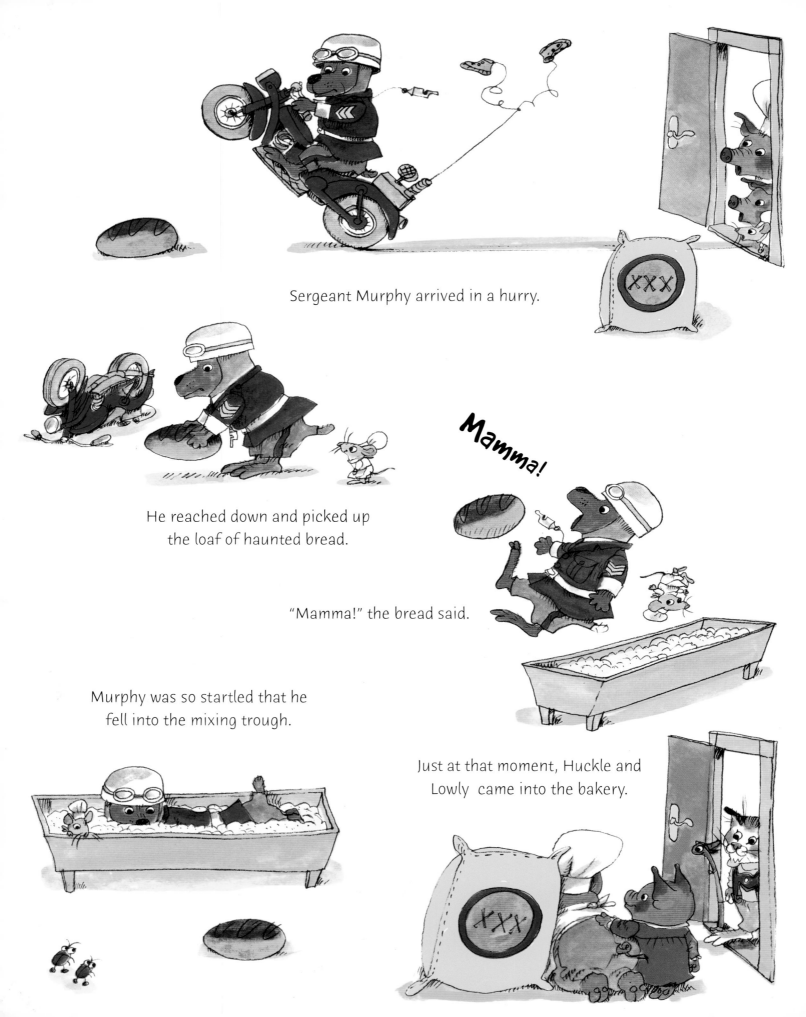

Sergeant Murphy arrived in a hurry.

He reached down and picked up
the loaf of haunted bread.

"Mamma!" the bread said.

Murphy was so startled that he
fell into the mixing trough.

Mamma!

Just at that moment, Huckle and
Lowly came into the bakery.

"That is a *very* strange loaf of bread," said Lowly.
Stretching out, he slowly ooched across the floor towards it.

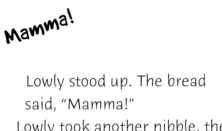

He took a nibble. The bread said nothing.

Mamma!

Lowly stood up. The bread said, "Mamma!"
Lowly took another nibble, then stuck out his head. "I have solved the mystery," he said. "Break the loaf open very gently, but *please*… don't break me!"

Humperdink gently broke open the bread and inside was…Flossie's DOLL!
It had fallen into the mixing trough and had been baked inside the bread.

With the mystery solved, they all sat down to eat the haunted bread. All of them, that is, except Lowly. He had already eaten his fill.

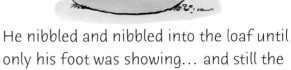

He nibbled and nibbled into the loaf until only his foot was showing… and still the bread said nothing.

Mamma!
Baby!

All right, Lowly! Please take your foot off the table!

Absent-Minded Mr. Rabbit

Mr. Rabbit walked down the street. He wasn't looking at the workmen, who were making a new, hot, sticky, gooey street. No! He was looking at his newspaper.

He wasn't looking at his feet, which were getting hot and sticky and gooey, too. No! He was looking at his newspaper.

Then suddenly he stopped looking at his newspaper. He looked down at his feet instead. And do you know what he saw? He saw that he was STUCK in that hot, sticky, gooey street!

The workmen got a long pole and tried to poke him out. It didn't work.

A truck tried to pull him out with a rope. No good! He was stuck all right!

They tried to blow him out with a huge fan. The fan blew off his hat and coat…
     but Mr. Rabbit remained stuck.

Some firemen tried to squirt him out. They squirted off his shirt
and tie – but Mr. Rabbit remained stuck. REALLY STUCK!
Well, now! He can't stay there forever! Somebody has
to think of a way to get him out.

Aha! Here comes a power shovel!
Let's see what it will try to do.

Well, the power shovel reached down… and scooped up Mr. Rabbit.

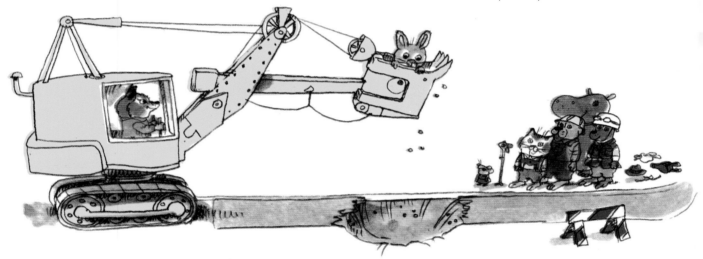

It dropped him gently to the dry ground. He would certainly have to
wash his feet when he got home, but at least he was no longer stuck.

He put on his clothes and thanked everyone.
As he was leaving, he promised that after this
he would always look where he was going.

But a little while later he was reading his newspaper again. He had forgotten his promise. And, naturally, he wasn't watching where he was going.

OH!!! DON'T LOOK!!!!

Sergeant Murphy and the Banana Thief

Sergeant Murphy was busy putting parking tickets on cars when, suddenly, who should come running out of the market but Bananas Gorilla. He had stolen a bunch of bananas, and was trying to escape.

Murphy! LOOK! He is stealing your motorcycle, too!

Sergeant Murphy was furious. Huckle and Lowly Worm were watching. Huckle said, "You may borrow my tricycle to chase after him if you want to."

B-r-e-e-e-t!

Away they went... chasing after that naughty thief.

They raced through the crowded streets. Don't YOU ever ride your tricycle in the street!

They crossed a drawbridge just as it was
opening to let a boat go through.

Bananas stopped suddenly and went into a restaurant.

Murphy said to Louie, who was the owner, "I am looking for a thief!"
Together, they searched the whole restaurant, but they couldn't find
Bananas anywhere.
Louie then said, "Sit down and relax, Murphy. I will bring you and
your friends something delicious to eat."

Somebody had better pick up those banana skins before someone slips on one.
Don't you think so?

Louie brought them a bowl of banana soup. Lowly said, "I'll bet Bananas Gorilla would like to be here right now."

"Huckle, we mustn't forget to wash our hands before eating," said Sergeant Murphy. So off they went to wash. Lowly went along, too.

When they came back, they discovered that their table had disappeared.

Indeed, it was slowly creeping away… when it slipped on a banana skin! And guess who was hiding underneath.

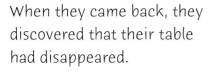

Sergeant Murphy, we are very proud of you! Bananas must be punished. Some day he has to learn that it is naughty to steal things which belong to others.

Speedboat Spike

Speedboat Spike liked to take his little boy, Swifty, out for a ride in his speedboat. Oh, my! Didn't Spike think he was the greatest!

Once he rammed into a sailing boat.

Another time he bumped into a barge and knocked a lady's washing overboard.
(Swifty! Why don't you tell your father to stop driving dangerously?)

Speedboat Spike just wouldn't slow down, and he wouldn't stop bumping into things.

STOP!

But that was before Officer Barnacle caught him… and made him stop!

Officer Barnacle ordered Speedboat Spike to keep his speedboat in a paddling pool UP ON LAND! Now Spike can go as fast as he likes, but he won't be able to bump into anyone.

POLICE

But who is that I see in that tiny little speedboat? Why, it's his little boy, Swifty! Oh dear! I think we are going to need another paddling pool. Go get him, Officer Barnacle!

Ma Pig's New Car

Pa Pig bought a new car to give to Ma Pig on her birthday.
She will certainly be surprised when she sees her new car, won't she?

On the way home, Pa stopped at a drugstore. When he came out, he got into a jeep by mistake. (You should be wearing your glasses, Pa Pig!) Harry and Sally thought that Pa had swapped cars with a soldier.

Stop, thief!

Then he went to the supermarket. When he came out he got into a police car. "You made a good swap, Daddy," said Harry. But Pa wasn't listening… and he didn't seem to be thinking very well either. Don't you agree?

Next he drove to a fruit stand to buy some apples. When he left he took Farmer Fox's tractor. My, but Pa is absent-minded, isn't he? "Ma will certainly like her new tractor," said Sally to Harry.

Then they stopped to watch a fire. When the fire was out they left – in the fire engine! How can *anyone* make so many mistakes?

Hey, Joe! You forgot to turn off the engine.

Then they stopped to watch some workers who were digging a big hole in the ground. No! Pa did NOT get into that dump truck. But by mistake, he got into...

…Roger Rhino's power shovel!
Ma Pig was certainly surprised to see her new CAR!
But, Pa! Do you know how to stop it?

Yes, he did!
Oh, oh! Here comes Roger now. He has found
Ma Pig's new car and is bringing it to her.
It looks as though he is very angry with that
someone who took his power shovel.

ROGER! PLEASE BE CAREFUL! You are squeezing Ma's little car
just a little bit too tightly. Well, let's all hope that Pa Pig will never
again make *that* many mistakes in one day!

The Three Fisherman

Lowly, Huckle, and Daddy were going fishing.

Their little motorboat took them far away from shore

Daddy said, "Throw out the anchor, Lowly."
Lowly threw the anchor out...and himself with it!

Lowly climbed back in and Daddy began to fish.

Daddy caught an old bicycle. But he didn't want an old bicycle. He wanted a fish.

Then Huckle fell overboard. Wouldn't you know that something like that would happen?

Daddy pulled Huckle out. Why, look there! Huckle has caught a fish in his pants!

Daddy fished some more, but he couldn't catch anything. He was disgusted. "Let's go home," he said. "There just aren't any fish down there."

As Daddy was getting out of the boat, he slipped… and fell! Oh, boy! Is he angry now!

But why is he yelling so loudly?

Aha! I see! A fish was biting his tail. The fish was trying to catch Daddy. It is good that Daddy has a strong tail. Now Lowly is the only one who hasn't caught…

Wow!

But look! Lowly has taken off his hat. Do you see what is under it? A FISH! Very good, Lowly.

Yes, there you see three very good fishermen!

The Accident

Harvey Pig was driving down the street.
(Better keep your eyes on the road, Harvey.)

Well! He didn't keep his eyes on the road and he had an accident.

B-r-e-e-e-t!

Sergeant Murphy came riding along. "Everyone get onto the pavement," he said. "I don't want anyone arguing in the street. You might get run over."
So everyone got onto the pavement.

And just in time, too! Rocky was driving his bulldozer down the street.
"I'm very sorry about that," he said. "I guess I wasn't looking where I was going."

All right, now. Keep calm, everybody!
Here comes Greasy George, the garage mechanic.

Greasy George towed away the cars, and the motorcycle, and all the loose pieces.
"I will fix everything just like new," he said. "Come and get them in about a week."

Greasy George worked and worked to make everything just like new again. Stand back, Lowly and Huckle! Don't get too close to him!

Well! Greasy George was certainly telling the truth. When everyone came back, everything was certainly NEW! I don't know how you did it, Greasy George, but I think you have the parts a little bit mixed up!

Please Move to the Back of the Bus

Ollie was a bus driver. All day long he called out to his passengers,
"Please move to the back of the bus."

At every single bus stop, he would politely say, "Please move to the
back of the bus. There are others who want to get on."

Look! See how his bus is filling up!

But look there! The back of the bus is empty. No one will move back.
Ah! Here comes Big Hilda. *She* will move to the back of the bus.

Big Hilda just managed to squeeze
on. By this time Ollie was furious.
"I am not going to drive any farther,"
he shouted, "until everyone moves
to the back of the bus!"

Does this bus go to Liverpool?

Oh, oh! Hilda *did* move to the back of the bus – and she moved everyone else with her!
Poor Ollie! Now he *couldn't* drive the bus any farther.
All right. Everybody out! This is the end of the line.

Uncle Willie and the Pirates

Not a soul dared to go sailing.
Do you know why? There was a wicked
band of pirates about, and they would
steal anything they could get their
hands on! But Uncle Willy wasn't afraid.
"They won't bother me," he said.

He dropped his anchor near a deserted island.
Aunty Pastry had baked him a pie for his lunch.
"I think I will have a little nap before I eat my pie,"
said Uncle Willy to himself.

Uncle Willy went to sleep. B-z-z-z-z-z.
What is THAT I see climbing on board? A PIRATE!
And another! And another? PIRATES, UNCLE WILLY!

But Uncle Willy couldn't do a thing.
There were just too many pirates.

First, they put Uncle Willy on the deserted island.
Then they started to eat his pie.
"M-m-m-m-m! DEE-licious!" they all said.

Uncle Willy was furious. He didn't care so
much about the pie, but he needed his boat if he
was ever going to get home again.
Then Uncle Willy had an idea. He gathered some
branches, some sea-shells, and some long beach grass.
He wove the beach grass into a kind of cloth.

Then he tied some sea-shells onto the branches and made a ferocious-looking mouth.

He tied the grass cloth onto the mouth, then attached some sea-shell eyes. By the time he tied on a spiky palm leaf, he had made a ferocious MONSTER!

Uncle Willy got inside. He was now "Uncle Willy, THE FEROCIOUS MONSTER." Look out, you pirates!

The Ferocious Monster swam out to the boat. The pirates were terrified.

They all ran into the cabin to hide.
The Ferocious Monster closed the door
behind them – and locked it.

The Monster had captured the wicked pirates!

Then the Monster sailed back home. Aunty Pastry
saw it from the dock. She was terrified!
"There is a horrible Monster coming!" she cried.
"He is even worse than the pirates!"

Uncle Willy landed, and took off his monster
suit. Everyone said, "Thank goodness it was
only you!" Sergeant Murphy took the pirates
away to be punished.

Well… Uncle Willy had made the seas safe
to sail on again. Hurray for Uncle Willy –
THE FEROCIOUS MONSTER!!!

How was the pie, Uncle Willy?

You BAD pie rats!!!

The Unlucky Day

Mr. Raccoon opened his eyes. "Wake up, Mamma," he said. "It looks like a good day."

He turned on the water. The tap broke off. "Call Mr. Fixit, Mamma," he said.

He sat down to breakfast. He burned his toast. Mamma burned his bacon.

Mamma told him to bring home food for supper. As he was leaving, the door fell off its hinges.

Driving down the road, Mr. Raccoon had a flat tyre.

While he was changing it, his trousers ripped.

He started again. His car engine exploded and wouldn't go any farther.

He decided to walk. The wind blew his hat away. Bye-bye, hat!

While chasing after his hat,
he fell into a manhole.

Then he climbed out and bumped
into a lamp post.

A policeman yelled at him for
bending the lamp post.

"I must be more careful," thought Mr. Raccoon.
"This is turning into a bad day."

He didn't look where he was going.
He bumped into Mrs. Rabbit and broke
all her eggs.

Another policeman gave him a ticket for
littering the pavement.

His friend Warty Warthog came up
behind him and patted him on the back.
Warty! Don't pat so hard!
"Come," said Warty. "Let's go to a
restaurant for lunch."

Warty ate and ate and ate.
Have you ever seen such bad table
manners? Take off your hat, Warty!

Warty finished and left without paying
for what he had eaten. Mr. Raccoon
had to pay for it. Just look at all the
plates that Warty used!

The lunch cost Mr. Raccoon every
penny he had with him. "What other
bad things can happen to me today?"
he wondered.

Well... for one thing, the tablecloth could catch on his belt buckle!

"Don't you ever come in here again!" the waiter shouted.

"I think I had better go home as quickly as possible," thought Mr. Raccoon. "I don't want to get into any more trouble."

He arrived home just as Mr. Fixit was leaving. Mr. Fixit had spent the entire day finding new leaks. "I will come back tomorrow to fix the leaks," said Mr. Fixit.

Mrs. Raccoon asked her husband if he had brought home the food she asked for. She wanted to cook something hot for supper. Of course Mr. Raccoon hadn't, so they had to eat cold pickles for supper.

After supper they went upstairs to bed. "There isn't another unlucky thing that can happen to me today," said Mr. Raccoon as he got into bed. Oh, dear! His bed broke! I do hope that Mr. Raccoon will have a better day tomorrow, don't you?

Lowly Worm's Birthday

It was Lowly's birthday.
Mother Cat was going to bake a birthday cake. Father was going to town to buy some eggs for the cake, and some candles to put on it. And maybe a few other things as well. "Be careful you don't break the eggs," said Mother.

Father Cat stopped at the hardware shop to buy some birthday candles. HE LEFT THE CAR ENGINE RUNNING!!! You know better than to do THAT, Father Cat!

Now! See what happened. The car drove off all by itself! I don't think Lowly knows how to drive. Anyway, he certainly doesn't have a driver's licence.

The car headed for the supermarket to get the eggs for Lowly's birthday cake. As it went past the egg counter, Lowly picked up some fresh eggs. Father Cat had to pay the cashier for them.

SOAP

pickles

SPECIAL
TODAY!
FRESH EGGS
IN A BASKET

They drove out through the back door of the supermarket.

They passed Mr. Fixit, who was fixing a broken traffic light. Hurry up and fix it, Mr. Fixit, before there is a bad accident!

Don't be a litter lout!

Hang onto those eggs, Lowly… and don't break any!

But where is Father Cat? Oh! There he is! He has just bought some balloons and favours at the party shop.

Through Farmer Alfalfa's hayfield they went. I don't think Farmer Alfalfa liked that.
But then… it was the car's fault. No one was steering it.

Father Cat was still chasing after them. He stopped for a moment in order to
buy some of Mrs. Alfalfa's delicious fresh strawberries. He thought they would
look very nice on Lowly's birthday cake.

At last they all came to a stop in Mother Cat's kitchen!

My babies!
My Lowly!

Lowly hadn't broken a *single* egg!

Mother Cat baked a huge birthday cake, and guess who
had the first bite! It was Lowly's most exciting birthday ever!
Happy birthday, dear Lowly…Happy birthday to YOU!

Happy birthday, Lowly!

Mamma!

Baby!

RICHARD SCARRY

What Do People Do All Day?

a poet writing poems

an artist painting a picture   a story writer

a pretty model   a businessman

a photographer   a secretary   an operator

CAFE

THE NEWS

ABC

THE REMARKABLE BOOK SHOP
E. KRAMER, PROP.

a newspaper reporter

a book printer   a newspaper editor

a saleslady   a janitor

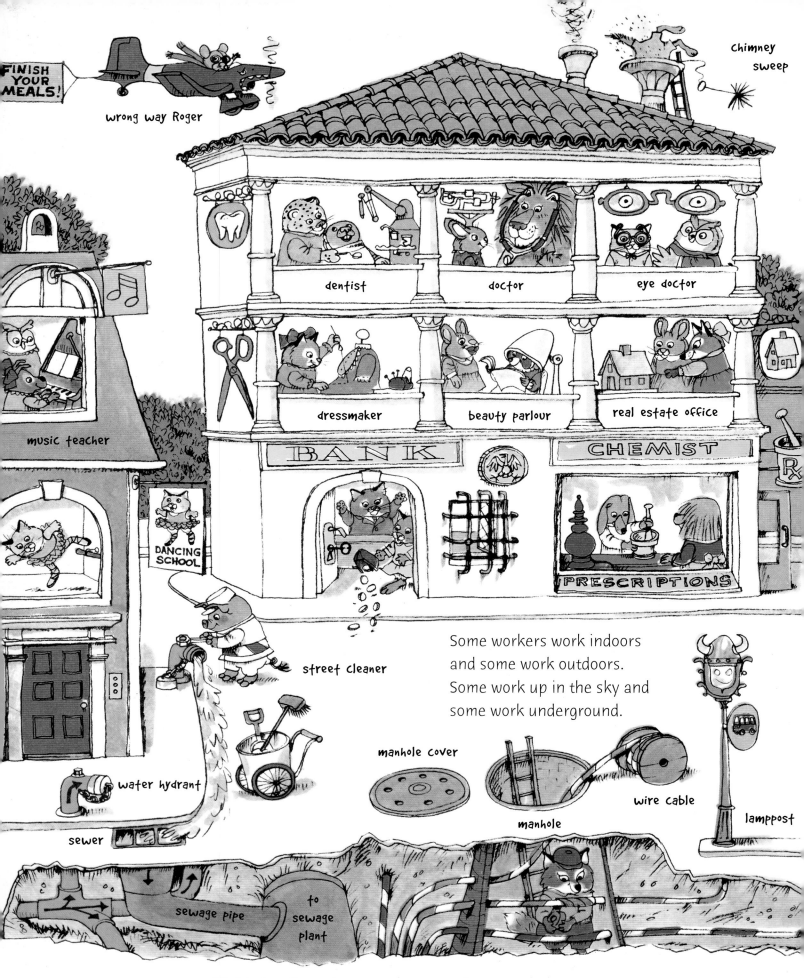

FINISH YOUR MEALS!

wrong way Roger

chimney sweep

dentist

doctor

eye doctor

music teacher

dressmaker

beauty parlour

real estate office

BANK

CHEMIST

DANCING SCHOOL

PRESCRIPTIONS

street cleaner

Some workers work indoors and some work outdoors. Some work up in the sky and some work underground.

manhole cover

water hydrant

manhole

wire cable

lamppost

sewer

sewage pipe

to sewage plant

All kinds of pipes and wires are buried underground

a stuck truck

FIRE STATION

RITZ MANSIONS

HARDWARE

window washer

BARBER SHOP

laundress

delivery boy

MOTOR CARS

car salesman

Some workers always do their
work at the same place.

Others travel from place
to place to do their jobs.

TELEPHONE
BOOTH

jack
hammer

What does your Daddy do?
What does your Mummy do?

TAXI

And what do YOU do?
Are you a good helper?

ditch digger

Everyone is a worker

Farmer Alfalfa

Blacksmith fox

Stitches the tailor Grocer cat Mummy Huckle

How many workers are there here?
One, two, three, four, five, six. What do these workers do?

Hi Daddy!

Farmer Alfalfa grows all kinds of food.
He keeps some of it for his family.

He sells the rest to Grocer Cat
in exchange for money.
Grocer Cat will send the food
to other people in Busytown.

GROCERIES

potatoes

Today Alfalfa bought a new suit with some of the money he got from Grocer Cat. Stitches, the tailor, makes clothes. Alfalfa bought his new suit from Stitches.

Then Alfalfa went to Blacksmith Fox's shop. He had saved enough money to buy a new tractor. The new tractor will make his farm work easier. With it he will be able to grow more food than he could grow before. He also bought some presents for Mummy and his son, Alfred.

Alfalfa put the rest of the money in the bank for safekeeping. Then he drove home to his family.

Mummy loved her new earrings. Alfred loved his present, too.

What did the other workers do with the money they earned?

First they bought food to eat and clothes to wear. Then, they put some of the money in the bank. Later they will use the money in the bank to buy other things.

What else did they buy?

Stitches bought an egg beater so that his family could make fudge. Try not to get any on your new clothes!

How do I look?

sand bag

bellows

forge

Blacksmith Fox bought more iron for his shop. He will heat and bend the metal to make more tractors and tools.

Grocer Cat bought a new dress for Mummy. She earned it by taking such good care of the house. He also bought a present for his son, Huckle. Huckle was a very good helper today.

Mother's work is never done

Good Morning! Good Morning! The sun is up! Everybody up! Wash! Brush! Comb!
Dress! Get up! There is a lot of work to be done!

Mummy and
Sally and Harry
made the beds.

They cleaned the house.

Mummy made
sandwiches
for lunch.

A brush salesman came to the door to sell brushes. Mummy didn't want to buy any brushes. My! He is trying very hard to sell Mummy a brush of some kind, isn't he?

Daddy came home from work and kissed everyone.

They sat down to supper. Daddy should know better than to try to take such a big bite.

After supper Mummy gave Sally and Harry a bath.

Daddy weighed himself on the scales. I think he has eaten too much.

Daddy read a story before bedtime.

Good Night!

He climbed up to kiss Sally goodnight.
Oh dear! I just KNEW he had eaten too much!

Are you all right, Daddy?

I don't think anyone will ever
sleep in that bunk bed again.
Do you?

Sally and Harry had to sleep with Mummy. What would we ever
do if we didn't have mummies to do things for us all day – and
sometimes all night? Good night! Sleep tight!

A voyage on a ship

Captain Salty and his Crew are getting their ship ready for a voyage.
The ship will carry passengers to visit their friends in a faraway land across the ocean.

At last the ship is loaded with the food and other things they will need on the long trip. Here come the passengers!

gangplank

They have all bought tickets for the trip. They give the tickets to the purser before they can go aboard the ship. NO PUSHING PLEASE!

light buoy

TOOOOOOOOOOOOOt!
It is sailing time. A tiny tugboat pushes the big ocean liner away from the pier. *Bon voyage!* The big ship sails out of the harbour.

Soon it is crossing the wide ocean.
There is no land in sight. Just look at all the
things that happen on an ocean-going ship!

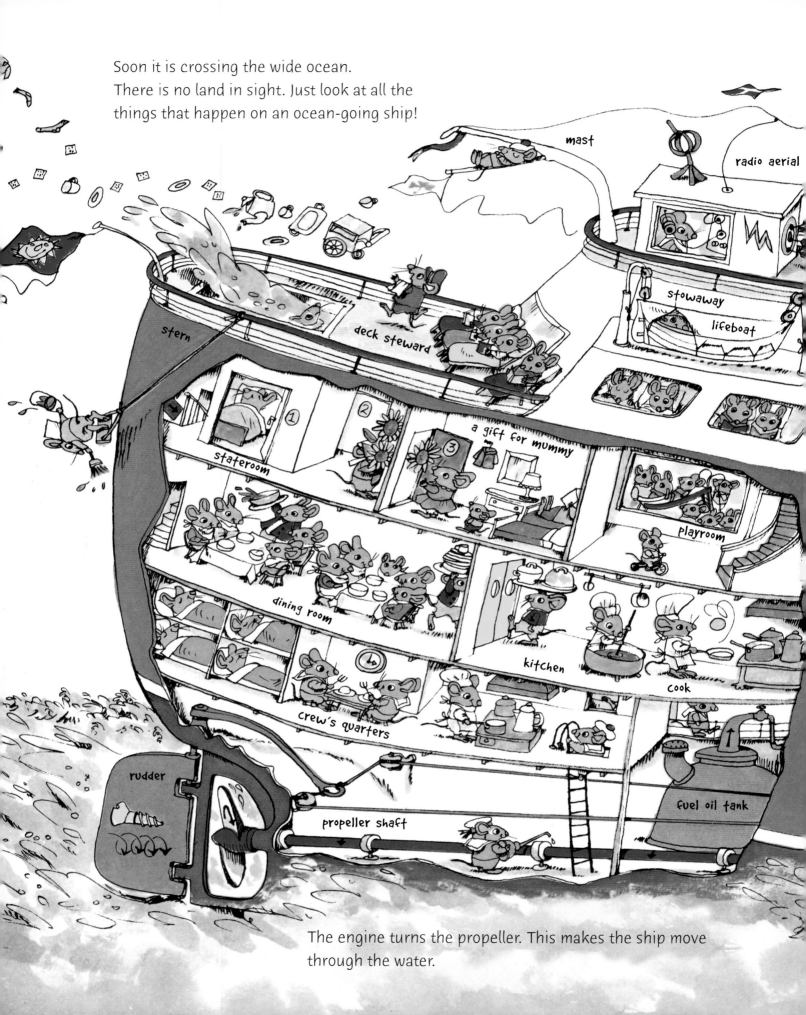

mast

radio aerial

stowaway

lifeboat

stern

deck steward

stateroom

a gift for mummy

playroom

dining room

kitchen

cook

crew's quarters

rudder

fuel oil tank

propeller shaft

The engine turns the propeller. This makes the ship move
through the water.

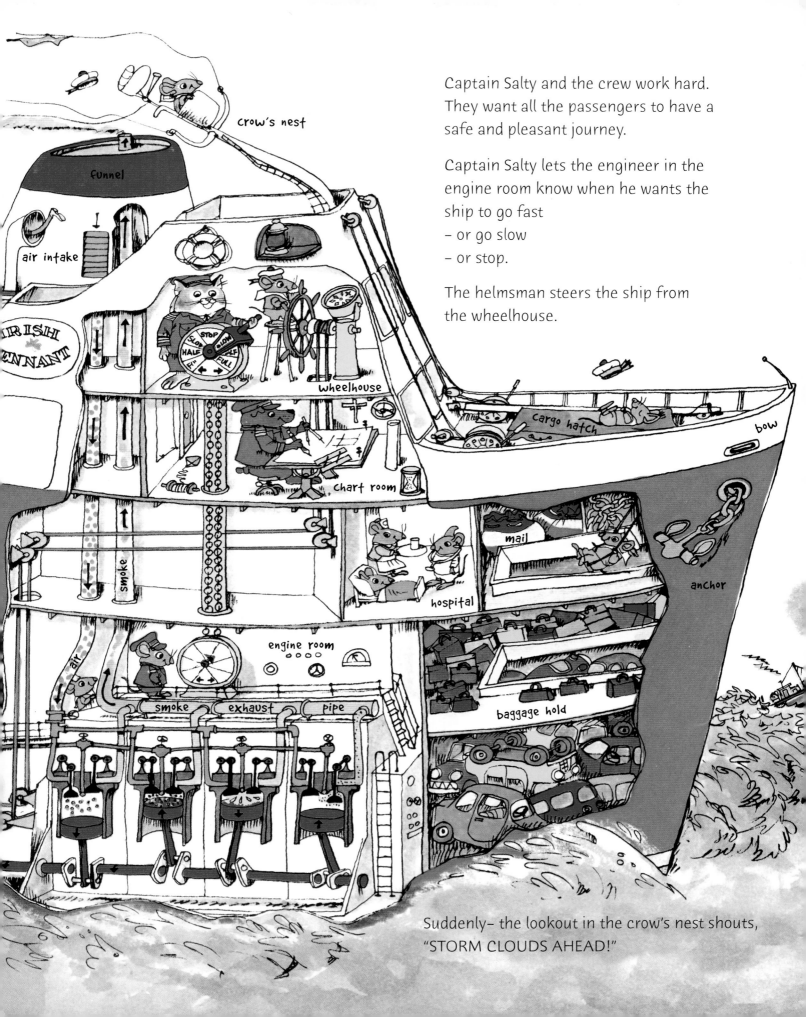

crow's nest

funnel

air intake

IRISH PENNANT

wheelhouse

chart room

cargo hatch

bow

mail

anchor

smoke

hospital

engine room

air

smoke   exhaust   pipe

baggage hold

Captain Salty and the crew work hard. They want all the passengers to have a safe and pleasant journey.

Captain Salty lets the engineer in the engine room know when he wants the ship to go fast
– or go slow
– or stop.

The helmsman steers the ship from the wheelhouse.

Suddenly– the lookout in the crow's nest shouts, "STORM CLOUDS AHEAD!"

The storm hits the ship with great fury!
The radio operator hears someone calling on the radio.
"SOS! HELP! SAVE US! OUR BOAT IS SINKING!"

Look! There it is! It's a small fishing boat in trouble!

"FULL SPEED AHEAD!"
roars Captain Salty.
My, the sea is rough!

LOWER THE LIFEBOAT!
Hurry! Hurry! The fishing boat is sinking!
Sailors Miff and Mo row to the rescue.

The boat sinks, but the fishermen are safe.

porthole

It's delicious!

Land Ho!!!

Back on board the liner, Captain Salty gives a party to celebrate the rescue. Will the storm never stop?

Then, just as suddenly as it started, the storm is over and the sea is calm. The ship continues on its journey.

Land ho! They have reached the other side of the ocean!

Everyone thanks the captain and crew for such an exciting voyage. Then they go ashore to visit friends. Other people have been waiting to cross the ocean to visit friends in Busytown. I wonder if their voyage will be as exciting as this one was?

Sergeant Murphy of the Busytown Police Department

Policemen are working at all times to keep things safe and peaceful. When Sergeant Murphy is sleeping, Policeman Louie is awake. He will protect the townspeople from harm.

Sleep tight!

Good Morning!

In the morning, Officer Louie goes home to bed and Sergeant Murphy gets up. Now Sergeant Murphy will watch out for everyone's safety.

At the Police Station the police chief tells Murphy to drive around town on his motorcycle. The chief can talk to Murphy over the radio if he has something important to tell him.

radio room

Keep everything peaceful!

radio

Chief

First, Murphy saves Huckle from drowning in the fountain..

Then he has to stop two bad boys from fighting.
Look Murphy! There are two more!

Just look at that traffic jam! What a mess! Murphy unscrambles it
and the street is peaceful again. Who is that in the Buffalo car?

O Ho! Wild Bill Hiccup and his Buffalomobile! He's speeding again!

He puts parking tickets on cars that are parked where they are not supposed to be.

Did you see that speeder hit Murphy's motorcycle? Chase him, Murphy!

Try to be good!

Murphy gives him a speeding ticket. For punishment he will not be allowed to drive his Buffalomobile for a few days. Let that be a lesson to you, Wild Bill Hiccup!

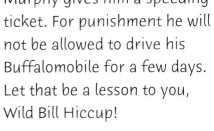

GROCERIES

I've been robbed!

catch the thief!

Now – guess what? Grocer Cat telephones the Police Station. A robber has stolen some bananas from the grocery store.

The chief of police calls Murphy over the radio. "CATCH THE THIEF!" he says.

catch the thief!

Look Murphy! There's the thief now!
It's Gorilla Bananas!

Murphy chases after him.
OOPS! His motorcycle slipped on
a banana peel. It is good that he is
wearing a crash helmet.

He has captured Bananas!

The police van comes to take Bananas to jail.
He will stay there until he learns that it is
wrong to steal things from others.

Nice work, Murphy!

It is time for Murphy to stop working. Now he can go home for supper with his family. Policeman Louie wakes up. He will keep everything peaceful during the night.

In the middle of the night, Louie hears a loud crying noise. If the noise doesn't stop it will wake up everyone in town. Why, it is Bridget, Murphy's little girl!
WAKE UP, MURPHY! BRIDGET IS HUNGRY!

Murphy has to get up and warm a bottle of milk for Bridget. Bridget stops crying.

Sergeant Murphy really knows how to keep Busytown safe and peaceful. Doesn't he?

Firemen to the rescue

FIRE!
Mother Cat was ironing one
of Daddy's shirts. The iron was
too hot. The shirt began to burn.
"FIRE!" she shouted.

Davy Dog went to the Fire-alarm Box.
He pulled the knob that sounded the
alarm at the fire station.

Firemen are at the fire station at all times.
They have to be ready to put fires out quickly.

As soon as the alarm rang, they ran to
their fire engines. HURRY!

Clang! Clang! Clang!
The firemen rushed to the fire.
They raised the ladder on the ladder
truck. A fireman ran up the ladder to
rescue Mummy. "SAVE MY HUCKLE!"
she screamed.

ALARM BOX

RESCUE-10

pumper engine

CHIEF

water hydrant

CHIEF

Save Huckle too!

Water is used to put fires out. The water runs through the pipes under the street.
The firemen attached a hose between the water hydrant and the pumper engine.
The pumper engine got water from the hydrant and squirted it out through the
hose nozzle.

But the ladder wasn't long
enough to reach Huckle up
in the playroom!
How will they ever save him?

"SAVE MY HUCKLE!" screamed Mummy Cat as the firemen carried her down.

Smokey came running to the house.
He had a smoke mask so that he would be able to breathe in the smoke-filled house.

He also had a special ladder.

He climbed up the fire-truck ladder as far as he could. He reached up with his special ladder and hooked it over the window sill. Then he climbed up. He just had to rescue Huckle!

The playroom door was closed. Smokey chopped it down with his axe.

He picked up Huckle – and he jumped out the window!

PLOPP!
Sparky and Snozzle were ready just in time to catch them in the life net. Daddy arrived just in time to see Smokey save Huckle.

At last the fire was out. Look at poor Daddy's shirt! But that doesn't matter. The firemen have saved his family and his house. That is much more important!

The firemen went back to the fire house.
They hung the wet hose up to dry.
They put a fresh, dry hose on the trucks.
They have to be ready to fight fires
ALL THE TIME!
Brave firemen are always ready to protect us and our homes from fire.

Hey! Smokey! Why didn't you just OPEN the playroom door?

A visit to the hospital

Mummy took Abby to visit Doctor Lion. He looked at her tonsils. "Hmmmm. Very bad tonsils," he said. "I shall have to take them out. Meet me at the hospital tomorrow."

On the next day, Daddy drove them to the hospital. Abby waved to the ambulance driver. Ambulances bring people to hospitals if they have to get there in a hurry.

Nurse Nelly was waiting for Abby. Mummy had to go home, but she promised to bring Abby a present after the doctor had taken her tonsils out.

Nurse Nelly took Abby up to the children's room.

Roger Dog was in the bed next to hers. His tonsils were already out. He was eating a big dish of ice cream.

Nurse Nelly put Abby on the bed. She pulled a curtain around them. No one could see what was going on.

Why, she was helping Abby put on a nightgown!

Doctor Lion peeked into the room. He told Nurse Nelly he was going to put on his operating clothes. He told Nurse Nelly to bring Abby to the operating room.

operating room

no germs | allowed

Off to the operating room they went.
Doctor Lion was waiting there. Everyone but the
patient wears a face mask in the operating room
so that germs won't spread.

Doctor Lion told Abby that she was going to
go to sleep. He said she would stay asleep until
her tonsils were out.

Doctor Dog put a mask over her nose
and mouth. She breathed in and out. In an
instant she was asleep.

When she woke up she found herself
back in the bed next to Roger's. Her
tonsils were all gone! Her throat was
sore, but it felt better after she had
some ice cream.

whooooeeee!

Abby saw her Mummy arriving in the
ambulance. Abby thought her mother
must be in a hurry to see her.

Hurry!

She waited and waited – but Mummy didn't come. At last Doctor Lion came. "Your Mother has brought you a present," he said. He took Abby for a ride in a wheelchair.

NURSERY

"There is your present," he said. "It is your new baby brother! Your Mother just gave birth to him here in the hospital." Then they all went to Mummy's room in the hospital. Daddy was there, too.

He looks like me, don't you think?

What a lucky girl she was! She left her tonsils at the hospital, but she brought home a lovely baby brother. But remember! Very few children receive such a nice present when they have their tonsils out!

The train trip

The Pig family is going on a train to visit their cousins in a town far away. They will travel all day and all night to get there.

Daddy buys train tickets at the railway station.

Mummy buys books and magazines to read.

A porter takes their bags to the train.

This old train has a steam engine.
It is only going to make a short trip to the next town.
The Pig family will ride overnight on another train.

Their train has a sleeping car with separate rooms for each family. These rooms are called compartments. At night, the seats will be made into beds. Look! There is Huckle's family.

Food and water is brought to the kitchen in the dining car. The cook will cook their meals. The waiter will serve them.

ALL ABOOOOOARD!
It is time to leave. The train rolls out of the station. The signal light tells the engineer that there is a clear track ahead. He doesn't want to bump into another train.

signal tower

Mailbags and heavy baggage are put on the train. Some of it will be delivered to stations along the way.

The locomotive needs fuel oil to make its motors go. The motors turn the wheels so that the train can roll along the railway track.

The switchman can switch the train from one track to another. If he makes a mistake the train won't go to the right place.

The ticket collector takes the tickets. The tickets show that Daddy has paid for the trip.

In Huckle's compartment, the porter is getting the pillows and blankets ready for bedtime.

It is time to eat dinner. Cookie has already made the soup. He is trying to toss the pancakes from the side that is cooked to the side that is not cooked. You are not doing very well, Cookie!

The postman delivers a bag of mail to the railway station of a town they are passing through.

The watchman lowers the crossing gates before a train crosses a road. He doesn't want any cars to bump into the train. But Wild Bill Hiccup just HAS to bump into something!

Oh dear! The train has swerved and the waiter has spilled the soup!

While they are eating, the porter changes their seats into beds.

After dinner, everyone gets ready for bed.

Clickety clack, clickety clack.
The train speeds on through the night. The train crew won't
go to sleep until the trip is over. Cookie is still trying to learn
how to toss pancakes. Keep trying, Cookie.

WIENER
SCHNITZEL

It is morning when they arrive at their
cousin's town. Their cousins are at the
railway station to greet them.
I think they will have fun on their visit.
Don't you?

Wood
and how we use it

We couldn't live without trees. We get wood from trees. We use wood in many ways. Let's see how we get our wood.

timber!

The lumberjack cuts down the tree.

The branches are cut off the tree trunk.

The tree trunk is sawed into logs.

tree trunk

a seed

a one year old tree

log

This tree is almost 100 years old and is ready to be cut down.

The logs are put in a river to float downstream.

The forest ranger watches out for fires. A forest fire could burn down a whole forest.

Some trees are left standing. Seeds from these trees will fall to the ground. New trees will grow in place of the old ones that have been cut down.

The foresters also scatter seeds from helicopters.

Loggers ride the logs down the river. They try to keep the logs from getting jammed. Oh dear! The logs are jammed! Unscramble that log jam, loggers!

Good work, loggers!
You broke up the log jam. Now the logs can float to the sawmill and be sawed into boards.

TOM SAWYER'S SAWMILL

Water falling over a water wheel makes all the machinery work.

timber

timberyard

SAWDUST THE CARPENTER

BOAT BUILDER

FURNITURE

The logs are sawed into rough boards.

The rough wood is sawed into boards of different sizes.

scrap timber

FOOLSCAP PAPER CO.

straddle truck

This timber is stacked in the timberyard to dry. Many kinds of workers come to buy the timber they need for building things. Daddy pig has bought some timber to build a bookcase.

The paper makers use scraps of wood to make paper.

FOOLSCAP PAPER COMPANY

chipper

chemicals

digester

blower

beater

mixer

Wet wood pulp moves onto a wire screen belt. Water is removed by rollers and dryers.

dry end   drying   paper making machine   wire screen   wet end   wet wood pulp

a finished roll of paper

ABC PRINTERS

Some paper is used to make bags and boxes. Some is for making books. The paper used in this book was taken to the printing shop where books are made. The printer put the words and pictures on the pages.

The boat builder uses curved pieces of wood to make boats.

BOAT BUILDER

The furniture maker makes beds and chests and chairs.

Carpenters have a custom of nailing a tree branch to the roof of a new house.

Some trees give us fruit.

Harry is planting an apple seed. An apple tree will grow from the seed. It will take a long time. Someday YOU might like to plant a tree.

Trees shade us from the hot sun.

Digging coal to make electricity work for us

steam boiler

FRESH AIR
ENTER HERE

STOP   GO

Pick! Pick! Pick! Dig! Dig! Dig! The miners dig coal out of the coal mine under the ground.

Water seeps into the mine, and has to be pumped out.

Lifts raise and lower the miners and coal cars.

After the coal is dug out, wooden props are needed to hold up the roof.

The miners use picks and drills to break the coal into small pieces.

The seeping water collects in the sump.

sump

Many years ago, sunlight poured down on the plants and trees and helped them to grow. When these plants and trees died, they sank into the ground. Gradually they were changed into coal.

BURIED SUNLIGHT COAL MINE

THE TIPPLE

COAL

COAL

DIANE

The coal is brought up out of the mine to the tipple. Then it is loaded into railway coal cars.

Miners need fresh air. A fan blows out the stale air and fresh air rushes in.

The miners blast the hard, black coal with explosives.

stale air leaves this way

EXPLOSIVE

The loader loads coal into small coal cars.

TO THE TIPPLE

loader

By burning coal, we are able to make electricity work for us. The electricity lights our homes. That is why we call coal "buried sunlight." There is electricity in everything. But it is not useful to us until it is moving. Coal helps to make electricity move.

A train brings the coal to the electric power plant.

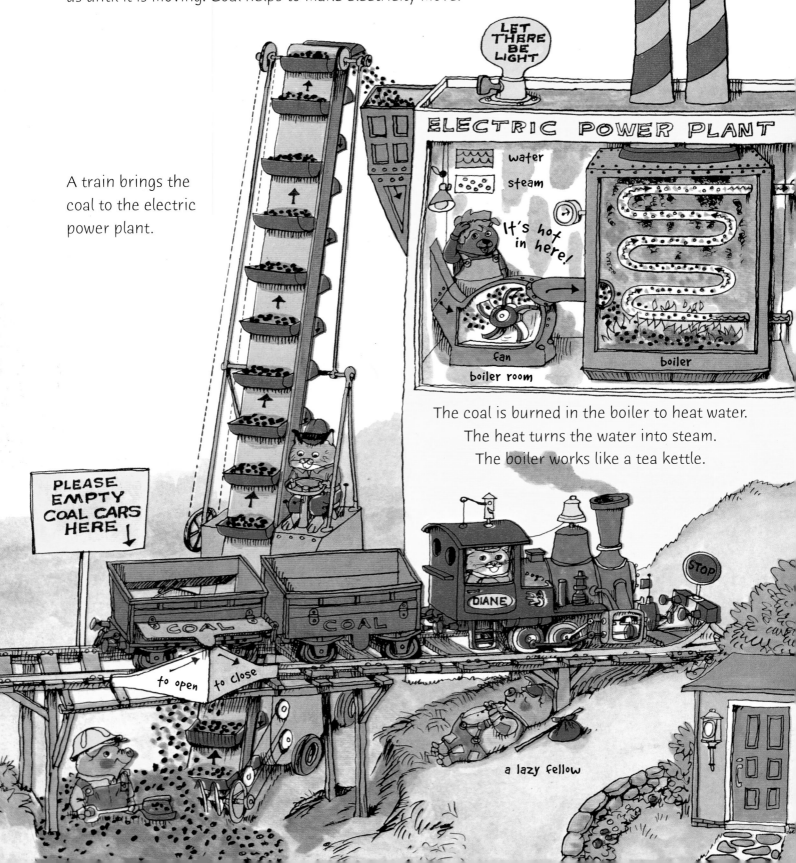

The coal is burned in the boiler to heat water.
The heat turns the water into steam.
The boiler works like a tea kettle.

The steam forces the turbine to turn, just as the wind moves a windmill. This turbine turns the electric generator that forces the electricity to move. This moving electricity is called an electric current.

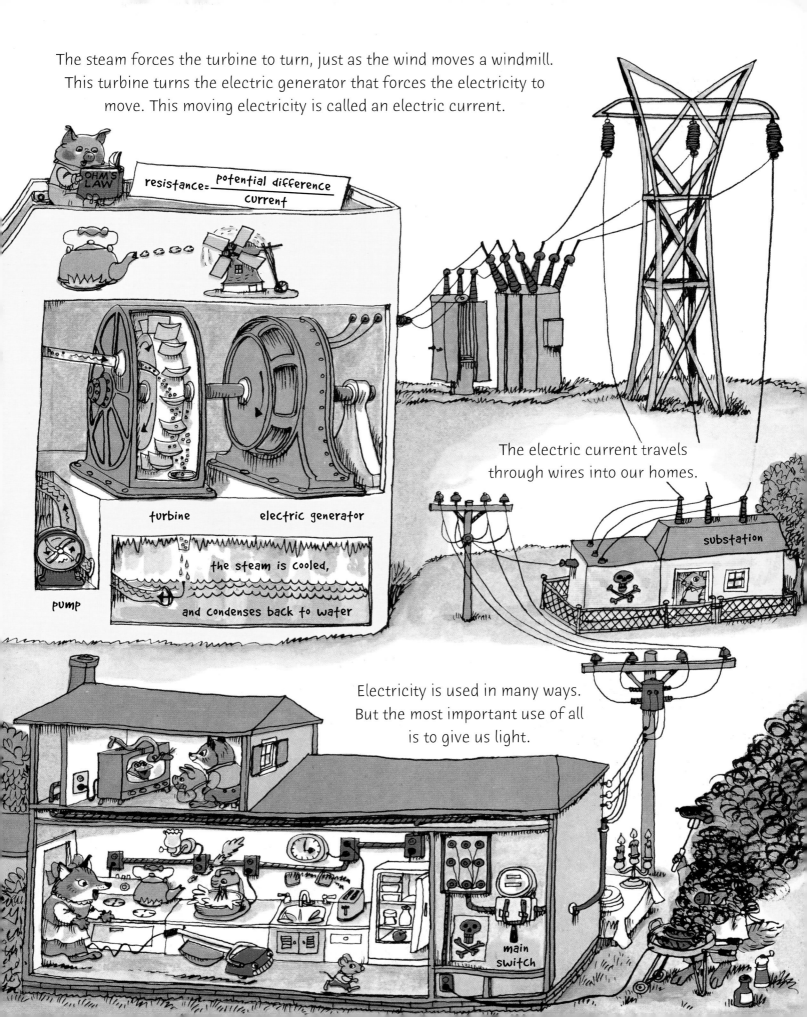

resistance= $\dfrac{\text{potential difference}}{\text{current}}$

turbine   electric generator

the steam is cooled,

and condenses back to water

pump

The electric current travels through wires into our homes.

substation

Electricity is used in many ways. But the most important use of all is to give us light.

main switch

Building a new road

Good roads are very important to all of us. Doctors need them to visit patients. Firemen need them to go to fires. We all need them to visit one another. The road between Busytown and Workville was bumpy and crooked and very dusty –

–except when it rained!
Then the dirt turned to mud and everyone got stuck.

The mayors of the two towns went to the road engineer and
told him that they wanted to have a new road.
The townspeople had agreed to pay the road engineer and
his workers to build the new road.

Get rid of those bumps! Make this road flat and straight, Bugdozer!

surveying instrument

BUMP

ROAD PLANS

The surveyor used his instruments to make sure that the road would be straight.

The motor crane lifts heavy things

The grader makes the ground smooth

The road builders used many machines to build roads. They put down big pipes to let streams of water flow under the road.

The bulldozer moves dirt

The surveyor's helpers used stakes and string to show where the road was to go.

water drainage ditch

tractor shovel

dump truck

ditch digger

At last the roadbed was straight and smooth. But it needed a hard top so that there would be no dust or mud.

power shovel

rock crusher

Big rocks were put into the rock crusher
to be crushed into smaller stones.

A stone spreader spread the
stones evenly over the roadbed.

ASPHALT
OIL
SPREADER

dump truck

stone spreader

A truck squirted sticky asphalt oil on the
stones to make them stick together.

keystone

The stone cuter shapes the stones
so that they will fit next to each other.

The asphalt mixer made hot, sticky asphalt.

The asphalt was poured into the level finisher, which spread it out flat on the road.

A heavy roller pressed down the asphalt to make it smooth and hard.

The road was built high in the middle so that rain water would roll off into ditches at the sides.

Street lights were put up so that drivers could see the road clearly at night.

FIREFLY LIGHTING COMPANY

electric cable

SNACK BAR

EAT

PETROL

PETROL & OIL

petrol pump

DIVIDING LINE PAINTER

petrol storage tank

GARDENER

OIL

All right you two fellows!
Stop talking and finish covering up that
underground storage tank!

The workers put up guard rails to keep cars from going off the road.

They posted many signs. Some signs remind drivers to drive safely. Some signs show which way to go.

A dividing line painter painted a line down the middle of the road. Dividing lines remind drivers to keep on their own side.

Don't push!

Everyone wanted to be the first one to drive on the new road. But Grandma Cat was the first! Wasn't she lucky?

HELP PREVENT FOREST FIRES

my mink

Water

We all need water. Nothing on earth can live without it. Even though we can't see it, there is a lot of water in the air. Sometimes it falls to earth as rain or snow. Then we can see it and feel it.

Now, let's see how we can make water work for us.

stream

water reservoir

water intake

dam

a picnic

ELECTRIC POWER STATION

electric generator

CROSS SECTION OF DAM

dam

A dam has been built across the river valley to hold the water back. After the water has been used in the electric power plant, it flows as a river down to the sea.

The wind turns the whirling vanes on the windmill. This causes buckets to lift water to feed the thirsty plants in the farm field up above the river.

Water lies in pools underground and can be pumped up for use.

river

The river water must be made clean and pure, so that it will be safe to drink. Water is pumped into the waterworks.

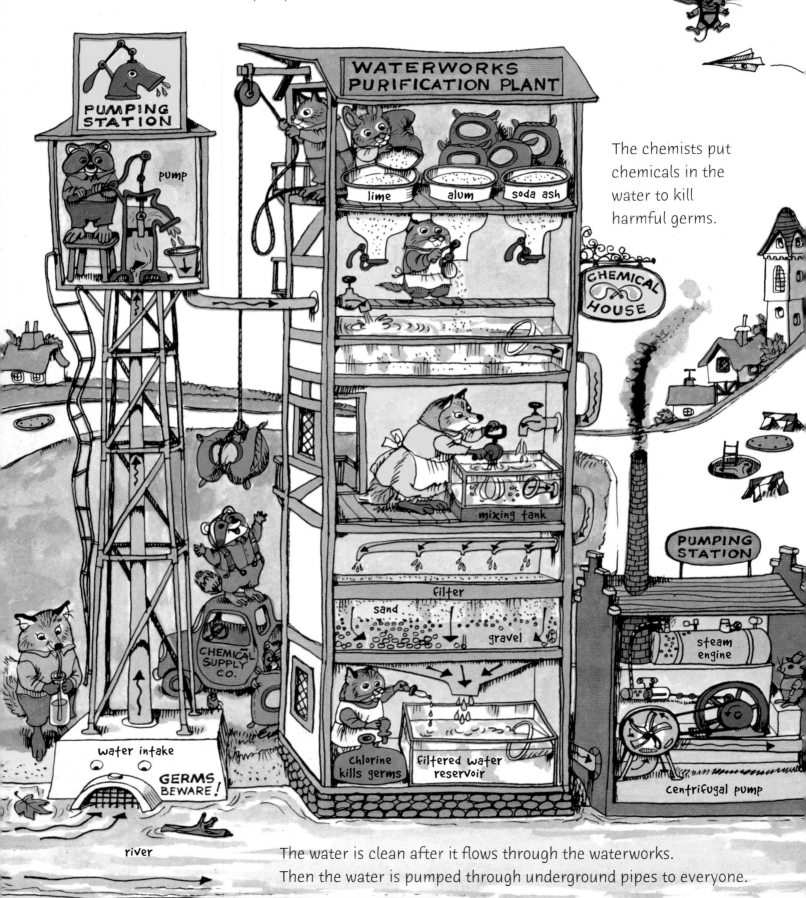

PUMPING STATION

pump

WATERWORKS PURIFICATION PLANT

lime   alum   soda ash

The chemists put chemicals in the water to kill harmful germs.

CHEMICAL HOUSE

mixing tank

CHEMICAL SUPPLY CO.

PUMPING STATION

filter

sand

gravel

steam engine

water intake

GERMS BEWARE!

Chlorine kills germs

filtered water reservoir

centrifugal pump

river

The water is clean after it flows through the waterworks.
Then the water is pumped through underground pipes to everyone.

river bank